DISCARDED

My Little Pony
Friendship is Magic
VOL. 15

WRITTEN BY **Heather Nuhfer**

ART BY **Amy Mebberson**

COLORS BY **Heather Breckel**

LETTERS BY **Neil Uyetake**

EDITED BY **Bobby Curnow**

 Spotlight   IDW

ABDOBOOKS.COM

Reinforced library bound edition published in 2019 by Spotlight, a division of ABDO, PO Box 398166, Minneapolis, Minnesota 55439. Spotlight produces high-quality reinforced library bound editions for schools and libraries.
Published by agreement with IDW.

Printed in the United States of America, North Mankato, Minnesota.
092018
012019

THIS BOOK CONTAINS
RECYCLED MATERIALS

Licensed By:

Library of Congress Control Number: 2018940477

Publisher's Cataloging-in-Publication Data

Names: Cook, Katie, author. Nuhfer, Heather, author. | Price, Andy; Breckel, Heather; Uyetake, Neil; Hickey, Brenda; Mebberson, Amy, illustrators.
Title: My little pony: friendship is magic / writers: Katie Cook; Heather Nuhfer; art: Andy Price; Heather Breckel; Neil Uyetake; Brenda Hickey; Amy Mebberson.
Description: Minneapolis, MN : Spotlight, 2019 | Series: My little pony: friendship is magic set 2
Summary: Welcome to Ponyville, home of Twilight Sparkle, Rainbow Dash, Rarity, Fluttershy, Pinkie Pie, Applejack, and all your other favorite ponies! When evil forces threaten the ponies' good life, it's up to the Mane Six to use the Magic of Friendship to face new challenges and conquer their fears.
Identifiers: ISBN 9781532142253 (v. 9; lib. bdg.) | ISBN 9781532142260 (v. 10; lib. bdg.) | ISBN 9781532142277 (v. 11; lib. bdg.) | ISBN 9781532142284 (v. 12; lib. bdg.) | ISBN 9781532142291 (v. 13; lib. bdg.) | ISBN 9781532142307 (v. 14; lib. bdg.) | ISBN 9781532142314 (v. 15; lib. bdg.) | ISBN 9781532142321 (v. 16; lib. bdg.)
Subjects: LCSH: My Little Pony (Trademark)--Juvenile fiction. | Hardware stores--Juvenile fiction. | Ponies--Juvenile fiction. | Fireworks--Juvenile fiction. | Dating--Juvenile fiction. | Love--Juvenile fiction. | Kings, queens, rulers, etc.--Juvenile fiction | Pirates--Juvenile fiction. | Book-worms--Juvenile fiction. | Libraries--Juvenile fiction. | Comic books, strips, etc.--Juvenile fiction.
Classification: DDC 741.5--dc23

Spotlight

A Division of ABDO
abdobooks.com

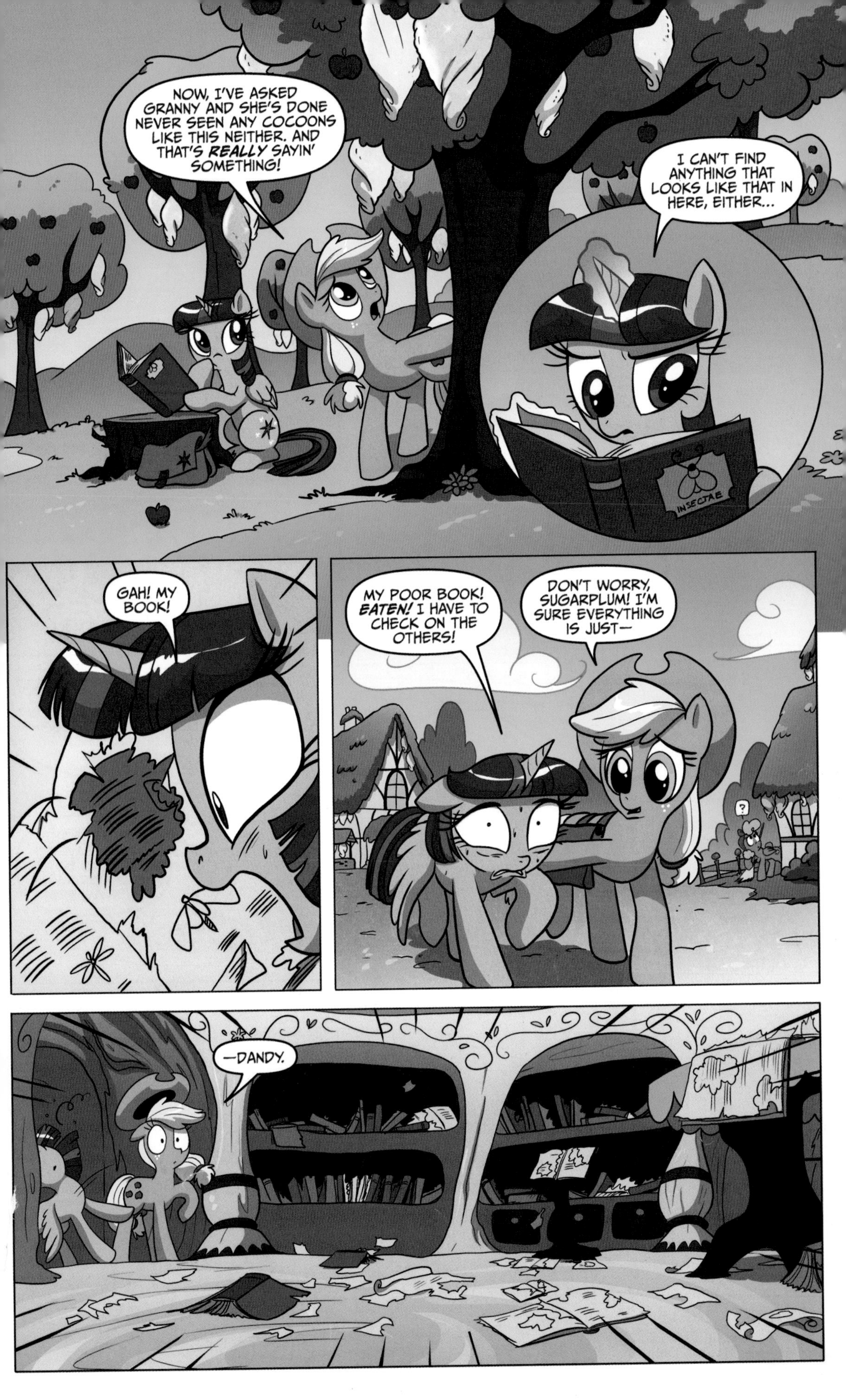
NOW, I'VE ASKED GRANNY AND SHE'S DONE NEVER SEEN ANY COCOONS LIKE THIS NEITHER. AND THAT'S *REALLY* SAYIN' SOMETHING!
I CAN'T FIND ANYTHING THAT LOOKS LIKE THAT IN HERE, EITHER...
INSECTAE
GAH! MY BOOK!
MY POOR BOOK! *EATEN!* I HAVE TO CHECK ON THE OTHERS!
DON'T WORRY, SUGARPLUM! I'M SURE EVERYTHING IS JUST—
?
—DANDY.

NO!

NO! NO!

NOOOOOOC

WHAT UP, MY PONAAAYS?

TURNS OUT TWILIGHT'S BOOKS MAY HAVE A BUG PROBLEM.

TALK ABOUT A VORACIOUS READER!

WELL, I GUESS YOU'VE GOT BIGGER PROBLEMS THAN I DO!

WHAT'S GOIN' ON?

SOOOOO, THERE IS A GIANT SCHMARFELPOD GROWING BY MY WINDOW AND I WANT TO THROW IT A COMING OUT PARTY, BUT I DON'T KNOW WHEN THAT WILL BE, *BUT* I THOUGHT YOU'D KNOW, APPLEJACK, SINCE YOU'RE ALL FARMY AND STUFF!

A "SCHMARFELPOD," PINKIE?

SURE! IT'S THE NAME I GAVE TO THOSE BIG BEANY THINGS GROWING EVERYWHERE!

GROWING *EVERYWHERE?!*

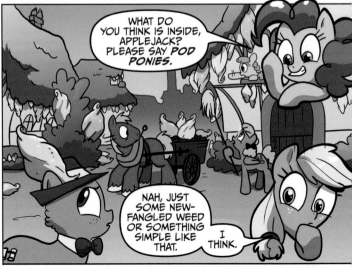

WHAT DO YOU THINK IS INSIDE, APPLEJACK? PLEASE SAY *POD PONIES.*

NAH, JUST SOME NEW-FANGLED WEED OR SOMETHING SIMPLE LIKE THAT.

I THINK.

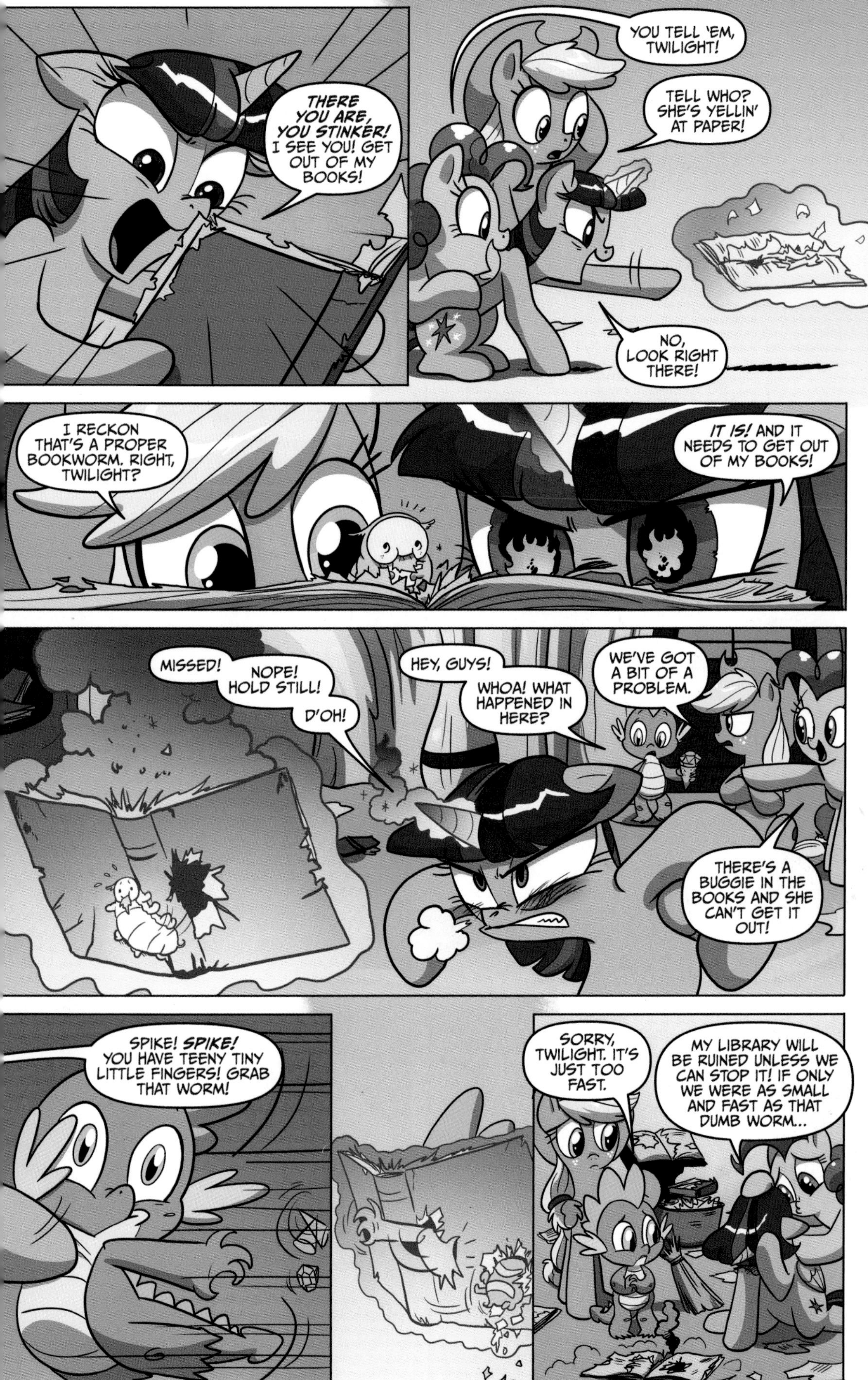
THERE YOU ARE, YOU STINKER! I SEE YOU! GET OUT OF MY BOOKS!
YOU TELL 'EM, TWILIGHT!
TELL WHO? SHE'S YELLIN' AT PAPER!
NO, LOOK RIGHT THERE!
I RECKON THAT'S A PROPER BOOKWORM. RIGHT, TWILIGHT?
IT IS! AND IT NEEDS TO GET OUT OF MY BOOKS!
MISSED!
NOPE! HOLD STILL!
D'OH!
HEY, GUYS!
WHOA! WHAT HAPPENED IN HERE?
WE'VE GOT A BIT OF A PROBLEM.
THERE'S A BUGGIE IN THE BOOKS AND SHE CAN'T GET IT OUT!
SPIKE! SPIKE! YOU HAVE TEENY TINY LITTLE FINGERS! GRAB THAT WORM!
SORRY, TWILIGHT. IT'S JUST TOO FAST.
MY LIBRARY WILL BE RUINED UNLESS WE CAN STOP IT! IF ONLY WE WERE AS SMALL AND FAST AS THAT DUMB WORM...

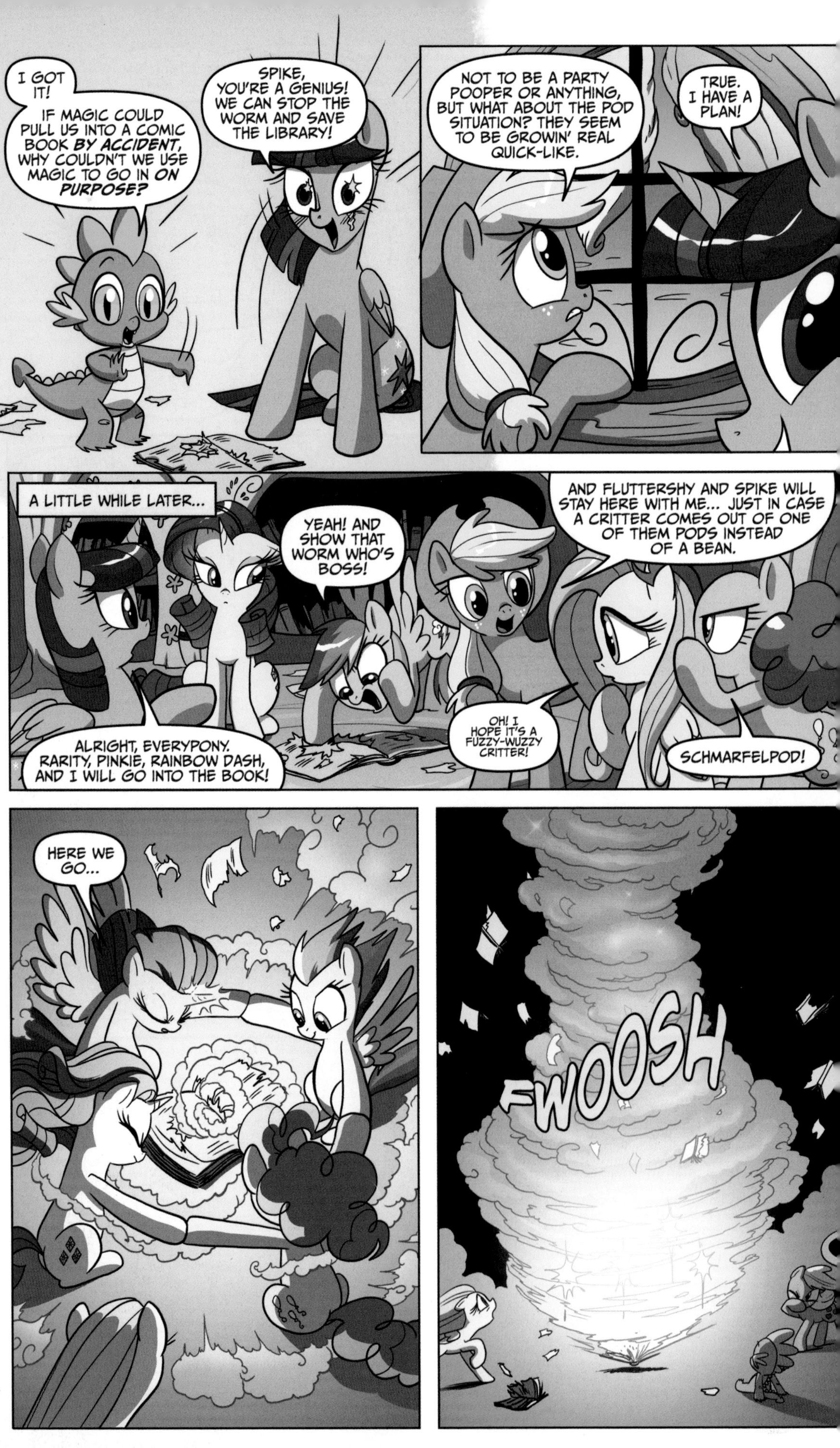
I GOT IT!
IF MAGIC COULD PULL US INTO A COMIC BOOK BY ACCIDENT, WHY COULDN'T WE USE MAGIC TO GO IN ON PURPOSE?
SPIKE, YOU'RE A GENIUS! WE CAN STOP THE WORM AND SAVE THE LIBRARY!
NOT TO BE A PARTY POOPER OR ANYTHING, BUT WHAT ABOUT THE POD SITUATION? THEY SEEM TO BE GROWIN' REAL QUICK-LIKE.
TRUE. I HAVE A PLAN!
A LITTLE WHILE LATER...
ALRIGHT, EVERYPONY. RARITY, PINKIE, RAINBOW DASH, AND I WILL GO INTO THE BOOK!
YEAH! AND SHOW THAT WORM WHO'S BOSS!
AND FLUTTERSHY AND SPIKE WILL STAY HERE WITH ME... JUST IN CASE A CRITTER COMES OUT OF ONE OF THEM PODS INSTEAD OF A BEAN.
OH! I HOPE IT'S A FUZZY-WUZZY CRITTER!
SCHMARFELPOD!
HERE WE GO...
FWOOSH

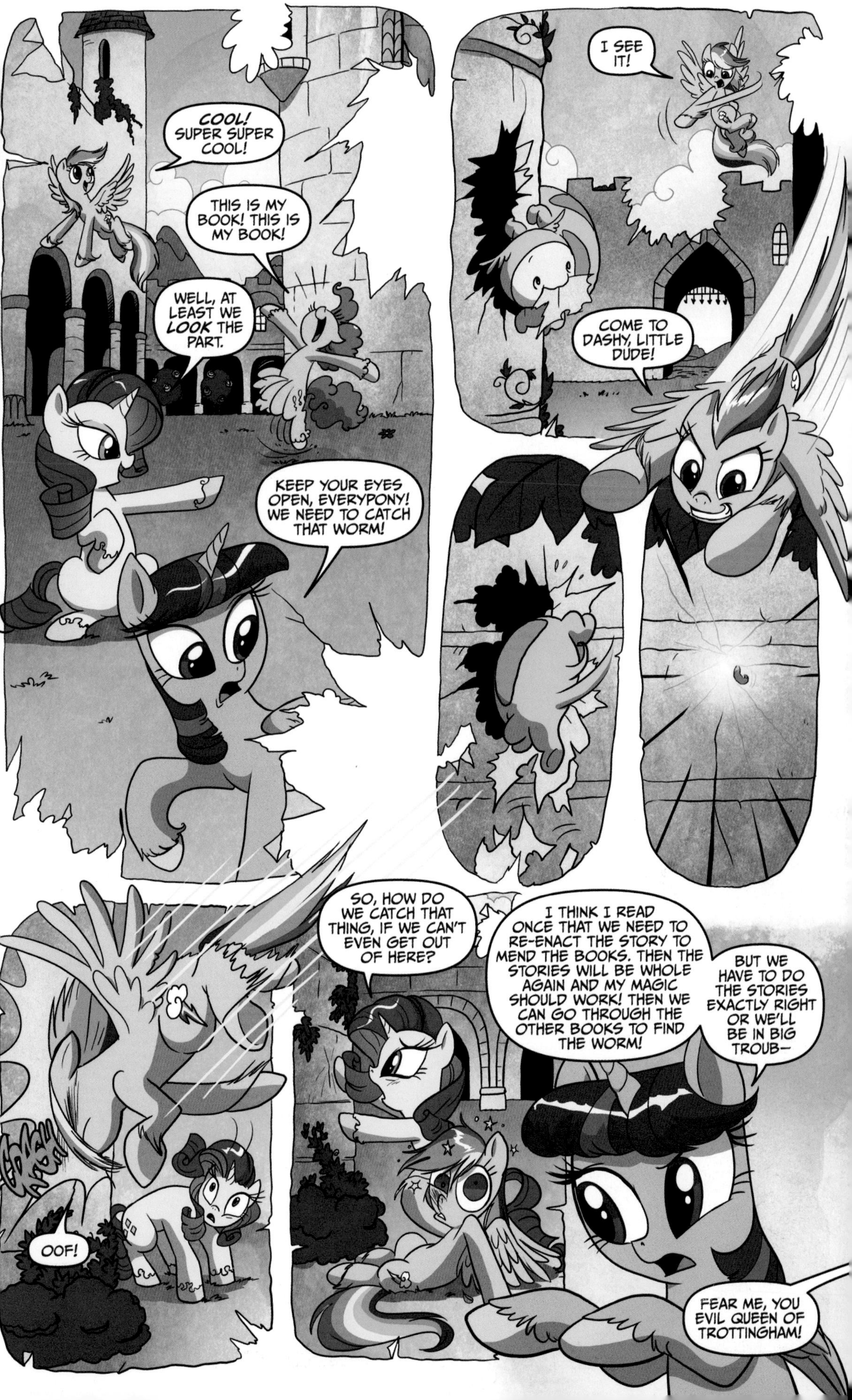

COOL! SUPER SUPER COOL!
THIS IS MY BOOK! THIS IS MY BOOK!
WELL, AT LEAST WE LOOK THE PART.
KEEP YOUR EYES OPEN, EVERYPONY! WE NEED TO CATCH THAT WORM!
I SEE IT!
COME TO DASHY, LITTLE DUDE!
OOF!
SO, HOW DO WE CATCH THAT THING, IF WE CAN'T EVEN GET OUT OF HERE?
I THINK I READ ONCE THAT WE NEED TO RE-ENACT THE STORY TO MEND THE BOOKS. THEN THE STORIES WILL BE WHOLE AGAIN AND MY MAGIC SHOULD WORK! THEN WE CAN GO THROUGH THE OTHER BOOKS TO FIND THE WORM!
BUT WE HAVE TO DO THE STORIES EXACTLY RIGHT OR WE'LL BE IN BIG TROUB—
FEAR ME, YOU EVIL QUEEN OF TROTTINGHAM!

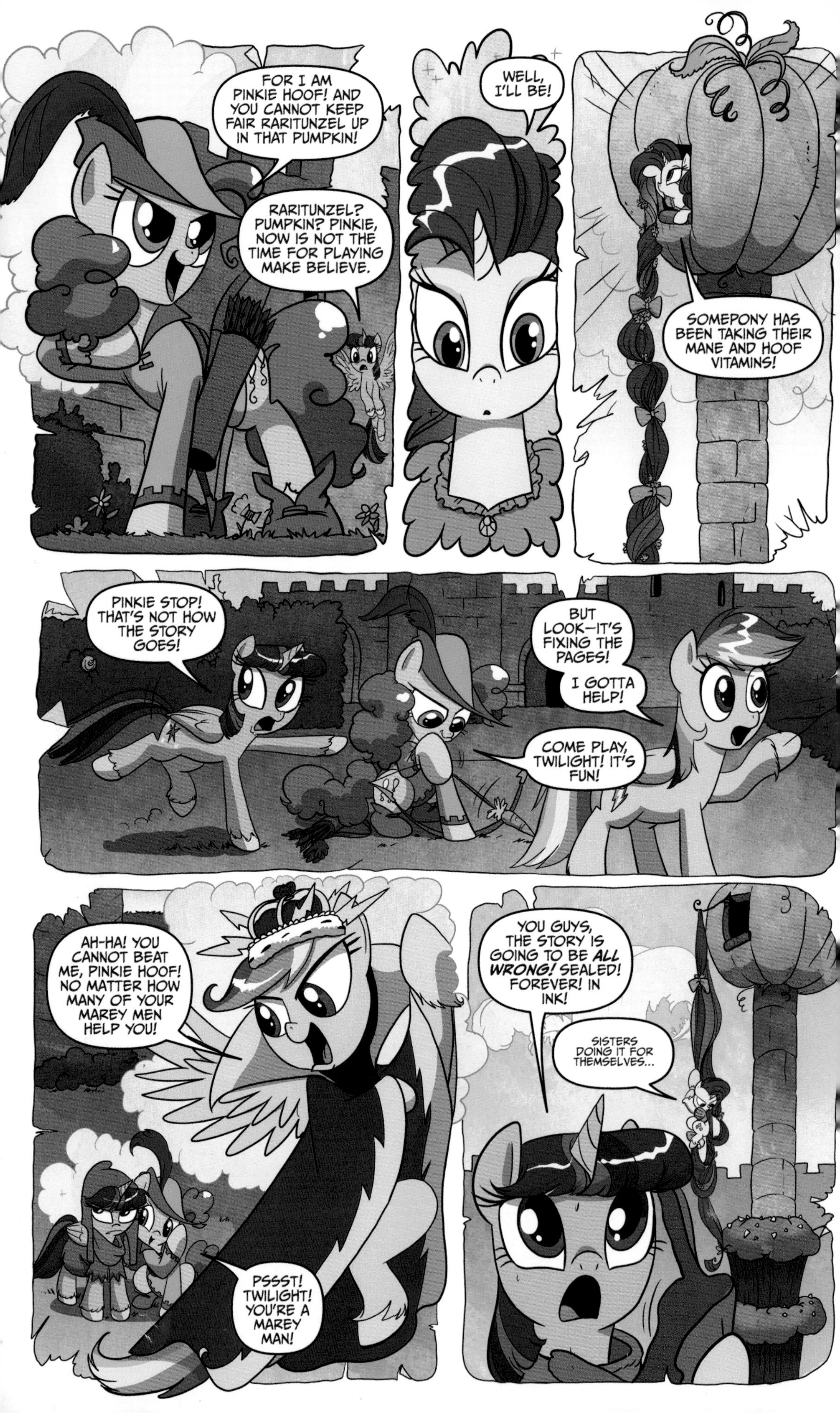
FOR I AM PINKIE HOOF! AND YOU CANNOT KEEP FAIR RARITUNZEL UP IN THAT PUMPKIN!
RARITUNZEL? PUMPKIN? PINKIE, NOW IS NOT THE TIME FOR PLAYING MAKE BELIEVE.
WELL, I'LL BE!
SOMEPONY HAS BEEN TAKING THEIR MANE AND HOOF VITAMINS!
PINKIE STOP! THAT'S NOT HOW THE STORY GOES!
BUT LOOK—IT'S FIXING THE PAGES!
I GOTTA HELP!
COME PLAY, TWILIGHT! IT'S FUN!
AH-HA! YOU CANNOT BEAT ME, PINKIE HOOF! NO MATTER HOW MANY OF YOUR MAREY MEN HELP YOU!
PSSST! TWILIGHT! YOU'RE A MAREY MAN!
YOU GUYS, THE STORY IS GOING TO BE ALL WRONG! SEALED! FOREVER! IN INK!
SISTERS DOING IT FOR THEMSELVES...

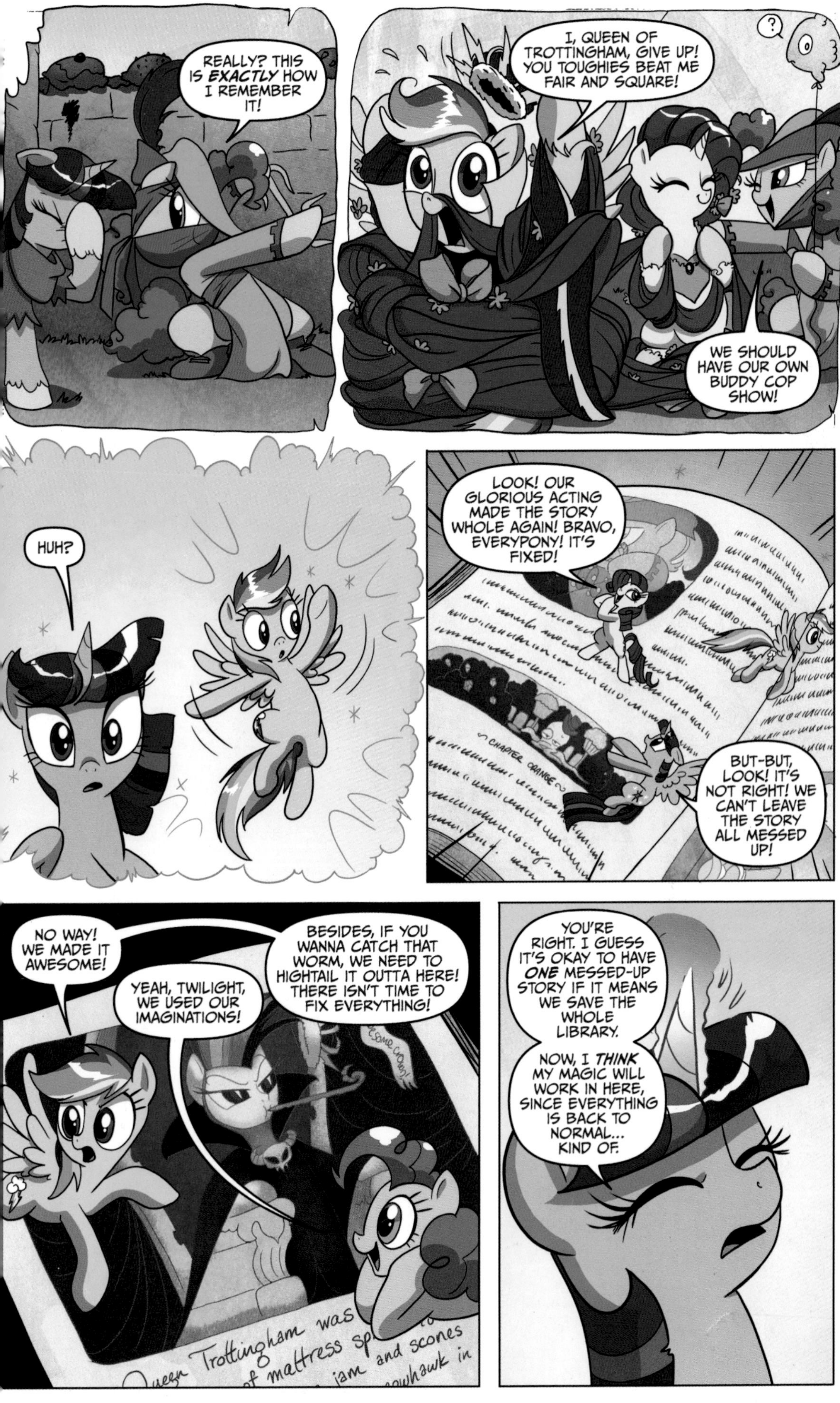

REALLY? THIS IS EXACTLY HOW I REMEMBER IT!
I, QUEEN OF TROTTINGHAM, GIVE UP! YOU TOUGHIES BEAT ME FAIR AND SQUARE!
?
WE SHOULD HAVE OUR OWN BUDDY COP SHOW!
HUH?
LOOK! OUR GLORIOUS ACTING MADE THE STORY WHOLE AGAIN! BRAVO, EVERYPONY! IT'S FIXED!
CHAPTER ORANGE
BUT-BUT, LOOK! IT'S NOT RIGHT! WE CAN'T LEAVE THE STORY ALL MESSED UP!
NO WAY! WE MADE IT AWESOME!
YEAH, TWILIGHT, WE USED OUR IMAGINATIONS!
BESIDES, IF YOU WANNA CATCH THAT WORM, WE NEED TO HIGHTAIL IT OUTTA HERE! THERE ISN'T TIME TO FIX EVERYTHING!
YOU'RE RIGHT. I GUESS IT'S OKAY TO HAVE ONE MESSED-UP STORY IF IT MEANS WE SAVE THE WHOLE LIBRARY.
NOW, I THINK MY MAGIC WILL WORK IN HERE, SINCE EVERYTHING IS BACK TO NORMAL... KIND OF.

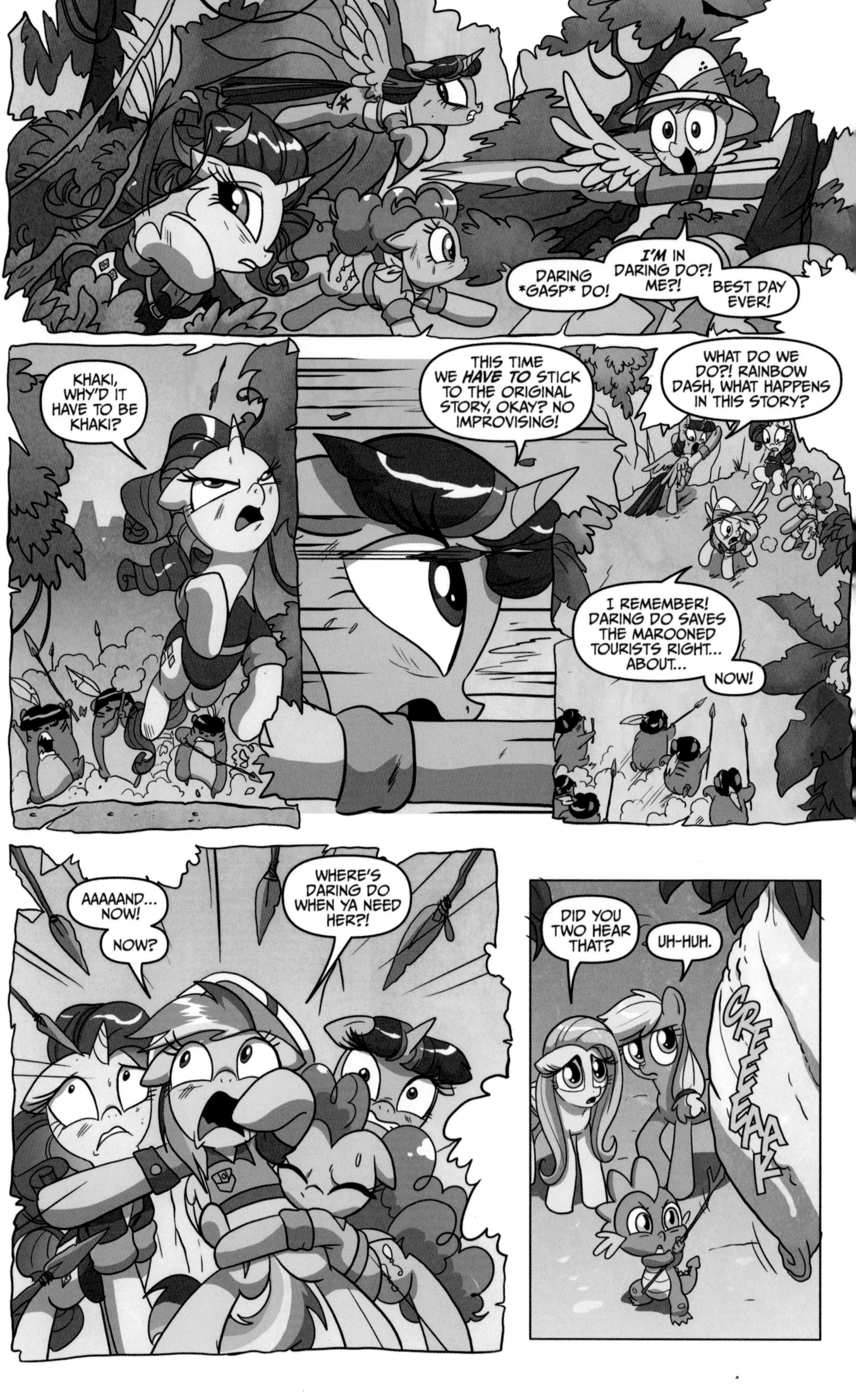

DARING *GASP* DO!
I'M IN DARING DO?! ME?!
BEST DAY EVER!
KHAKI, WHY'D IT HAVE TO BE KHAKI?
THIS TIME WE HAVE TO STICK TO THE ORIGINAL STORY, OKAY? NO IMPROVISING!
WHAT DO WE DO?! RAINBOW DASH, WHAT HAPPENS IN THIS STORY?
I REMEMBER! DARING DO SAVES THE MAROONED TOURISTS RIGHT... ABOUT...
NOW!
AAAAAND... NOW!
NOW?
WHERE'S DARING DO WHEN YA NEED HER?!
DID YOU TWO HEAR THAT?
UH-HUH.
CREEEAAAK

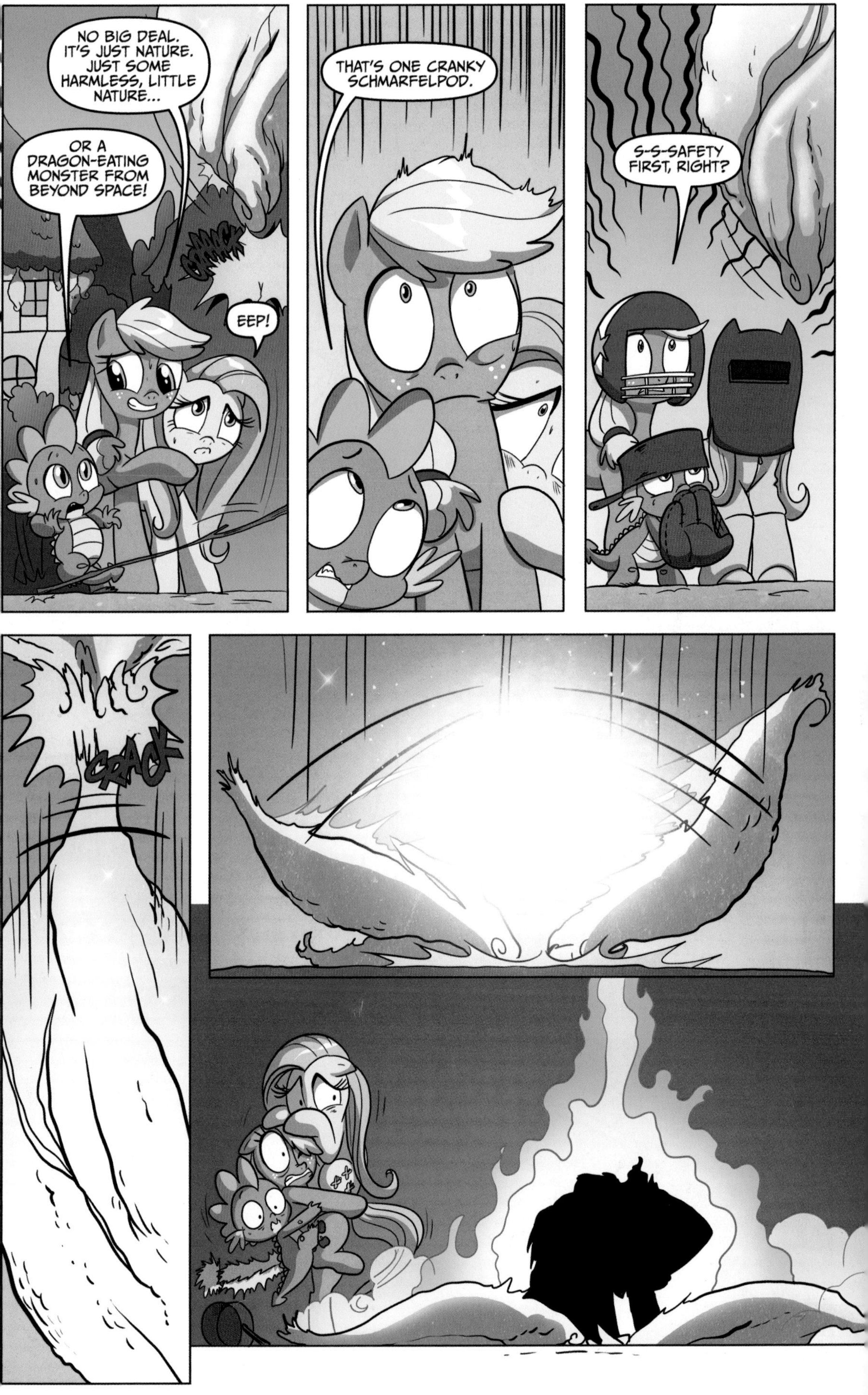
NO BIG DEAL. IT'S JUST NATURE. JUST SOME HARMLESS, LITTLE NATURE...
OR A DRAGON-EATING MONSTER FROM BEYOND SPACE!
EEP!
THAT'S ONE CRANKY SCHMARFELPOD.
S-S-SAFETY FIRST, RIGHT?
CRACK

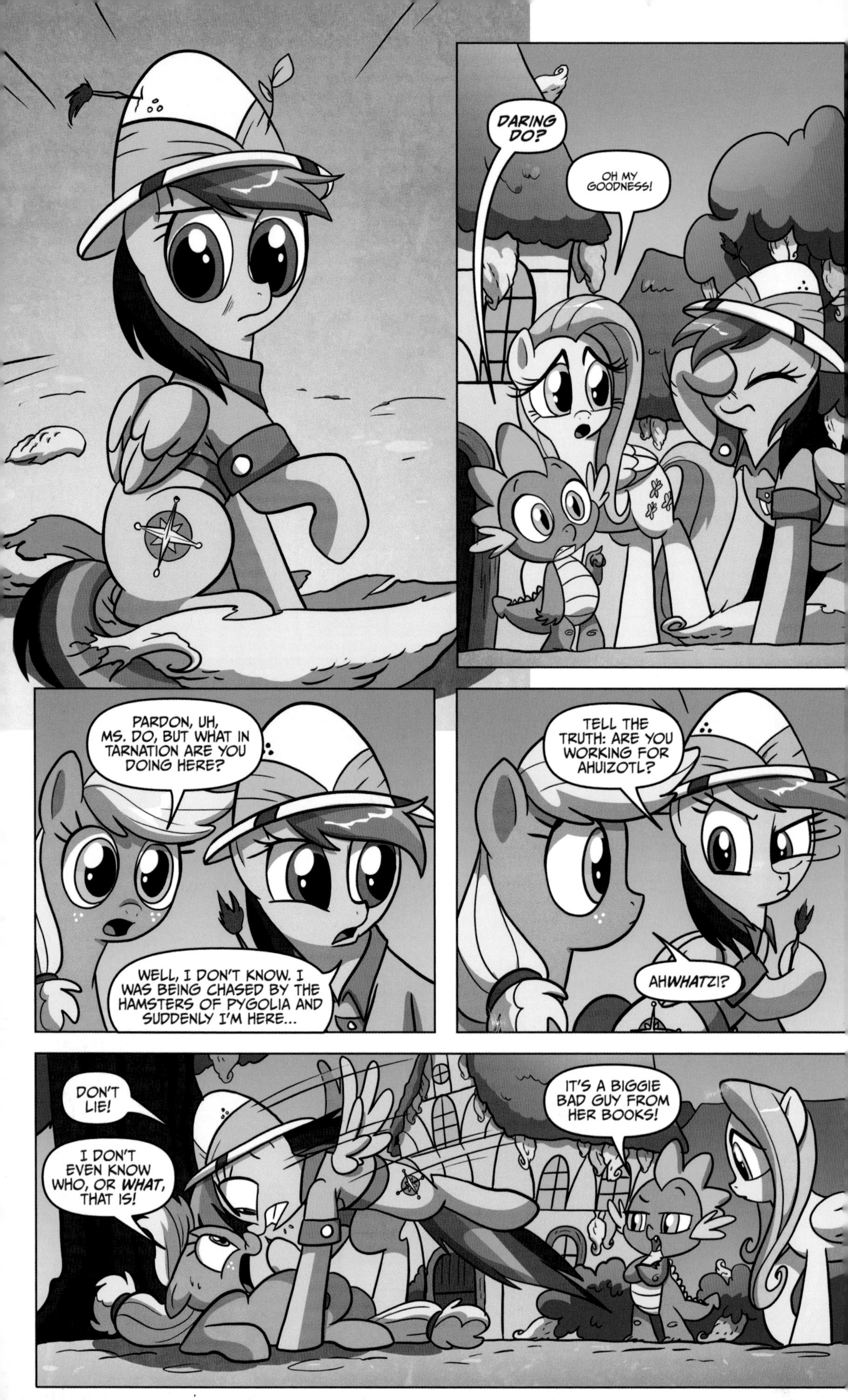
DARING DO?
OH MY GOODNESS!
PARDON, UH, MS. DO, BUT WHAT IN TARNATION ARE YOU DOING HERE?
WELL, I DON'T KNOW. I WAS BEING CHASED BY THE HAMSTERS OF PYGOLIA AND SUDDENLY I'M HERE...
TELL THE TRUTH: ARE YOU WORKING FOR AHUIZOTL?
AHWHATZ!?
DON'T LIE!
I DON'T EVEN KNOW WHO, OR WHAT, THAT IS!
IT'S A BIGGIE BAD GUY FROM HER BOOKS!

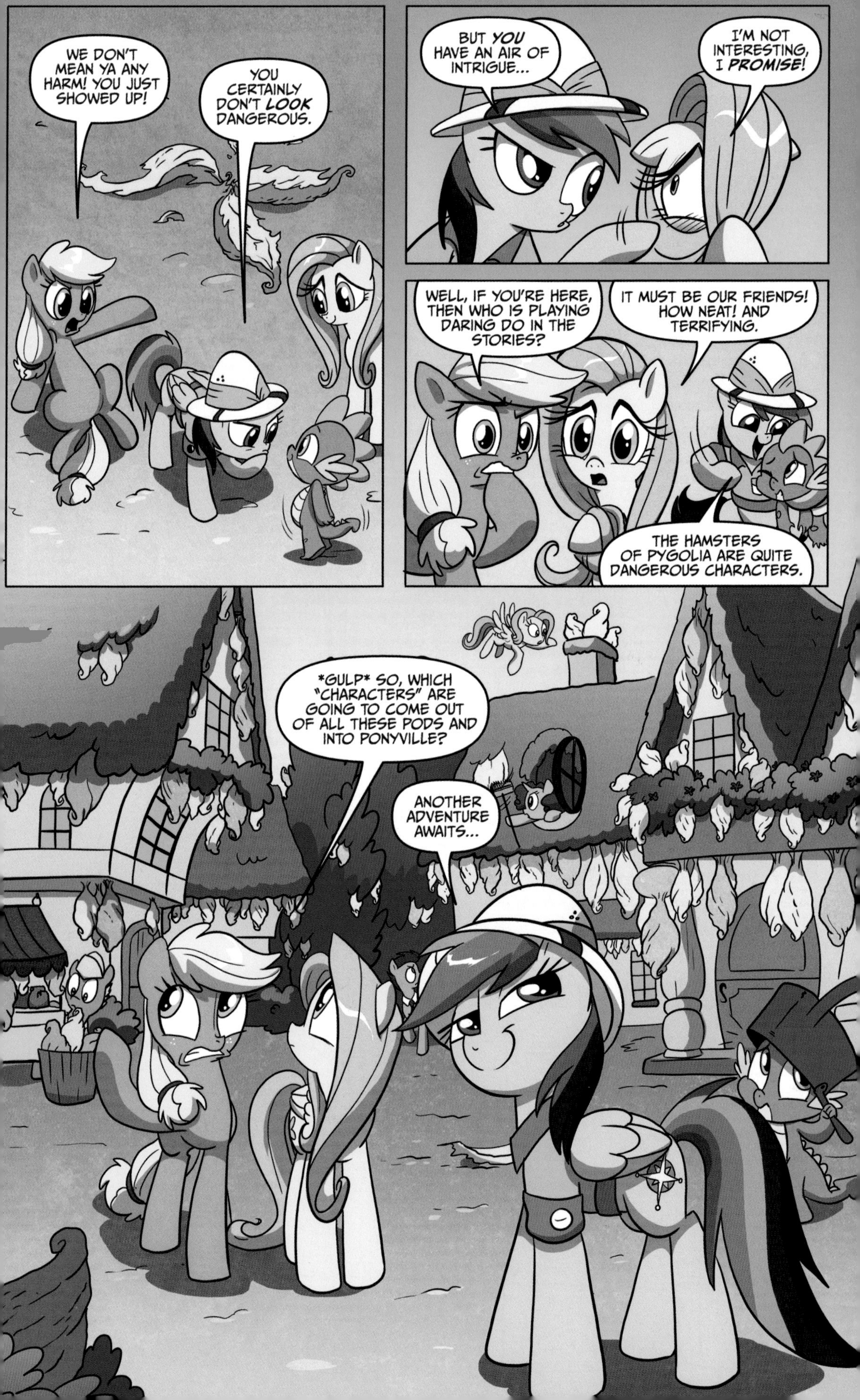
WE DON'T MEAN YA ANY HARM! YOU JUST SHOWED UP!
YOU CERTAINLY DON'T *LOOK* DANGEROUS.
BUT *YOU* HAVE AN AIR OF INTRIGUE...
I'M NOT INTERESTING, I *PROMISE*!
WELL, IF YOU'RE HERE, THEN WHO IS PLAYING DARING DO IN THE STORIES?
IT MUST BE OUR FRIENDS! HOW NEAT! AND TERRIFYING.
THE HAMSTERS OF PYGOLIA ARE QUITE DANGEROUS CHARACTERS.
GULP SO, WHICH "CHARACTERS" ARE GOING TO COME OUT OF ALL THESE PODS AND INTO PONYVILLE?
ANOTHER ADVENTURE AWAITS...

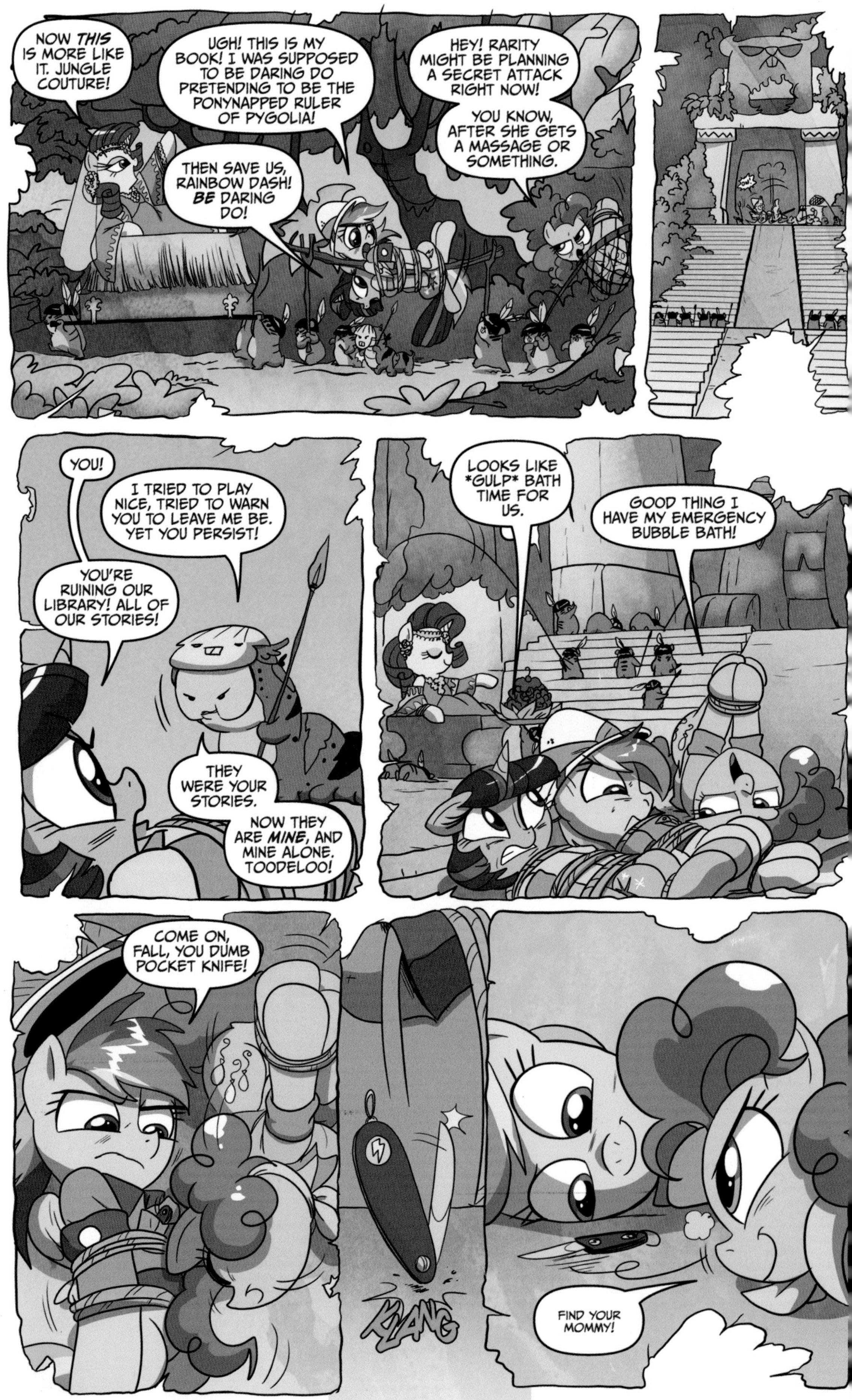
NOW THIS IS MORE LIKE IT. JUNGLE COUTURE!
UGH! THIS IS MY BOOK! I WAS SUPPOSED TO BE DARING DO PRETENDING TO BE THE PONYNAPPED RULER OF PYGOLIA!
THEN SAVE US, RAINBOW DASH! BE DARING DO!
HEY! RARITY MIGHT BE PLANNING A SECRET ATTACK RIGHT NOW!
YOU KNOW, AFTER SHE GETS A MASSAGE OR SOMETHING.
YOU!
I TRIED TO PLAY NICE, TRIED TO WARN YOU TO LEAVE ME BE. YET YOU PERSIST!
YOU'RE RUINING OUR LIBRARY! ALL OF OUR STORIES!
THEY WERE YOUR STORIES.
NOW THEY ARE MINE, AND MINE ALONE. TOODELOO!
LOOKS LIKE *GULP* BATH TIME FOR US.
GOOD THING I HAVE MY EMERGENCY BUBBLE BATH!
COME ON, FALL, YOU DUMB POCKET KNIFE!
KLANG
FIND YOUR MOMMY!

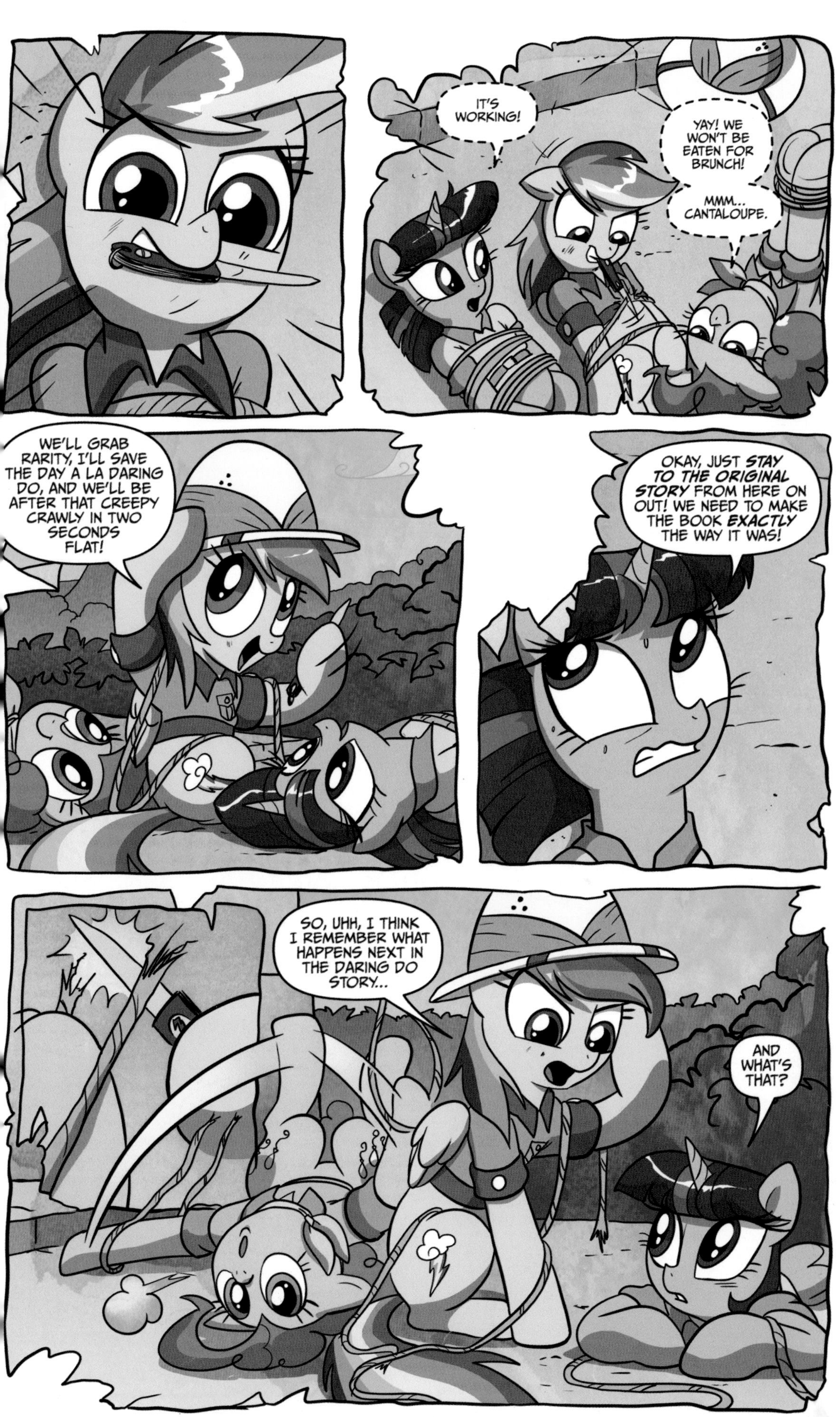
IT'S WORKING!
YAY! WE WON'T BE EATEN FOR BRUNCH!
MMM... CANTALOUPE.
WE'LL GRAB RARITY, I'LL SAVE THE DAY A LA DARING DO, AND WE'LL BE AFTER THAT CREEPY CRAWLY IN TWO SECONDS FLAT!
OKAY, JUST STAY TO THE ORIGINAL STORY FROM HERE ON OUT! WE NEED TO MAKE THE BOOK EXACTLY THE WAY IT WAS!
SO, UHH, I THINK I REMEMBER WHAT HAPPENS NEXT IN THE DARING DO STORY...
AND WHAT'S THAT?

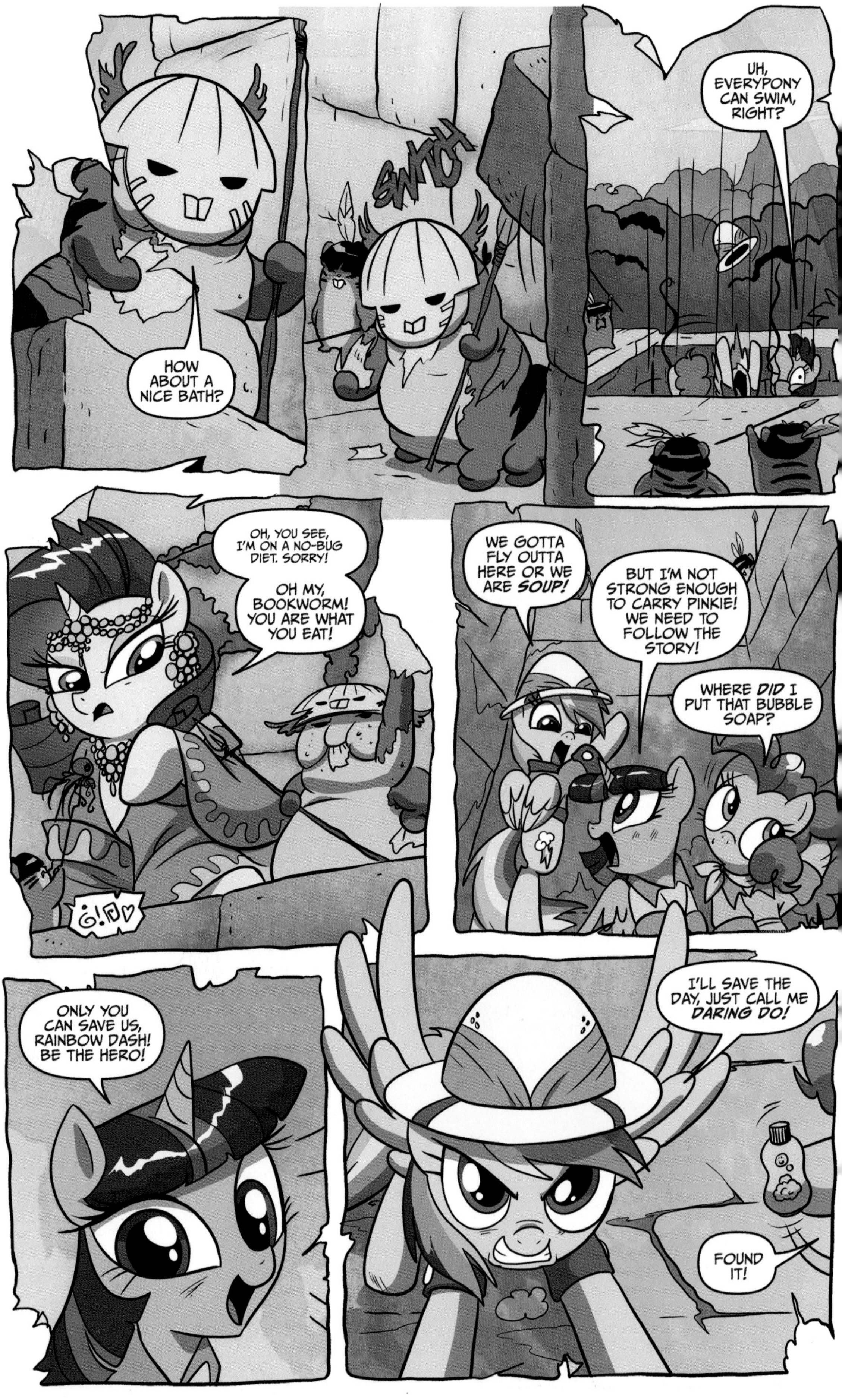

HOW ABOUT A NICE BATH?
SWTCH
UH, EVERYPONY CAN SWIM, RIGHT?
OH, YOU SEE, I'M ON A NO-BUG DIET. SORRY!
OH MY, BOOKWORM! YOU ARE WHAT YOU EAT!
WE GOTTA FLY OUTTA HERE OR WE ARE *SOUP!*
BUT I'M NOT STRONG ENOUGH TO CARRY PINKIE! WE NEED TO FOLLOW THE STORY!
WHERE *DID* I PUT THAT BUBBLE SOAP?
ONLY YOU CAN SAVE US, RAINBOW DASH! BE THE HERO!
I'LL SAVE THE DAY, JUST CALL ME *DARING DO!*
FOUND IT!

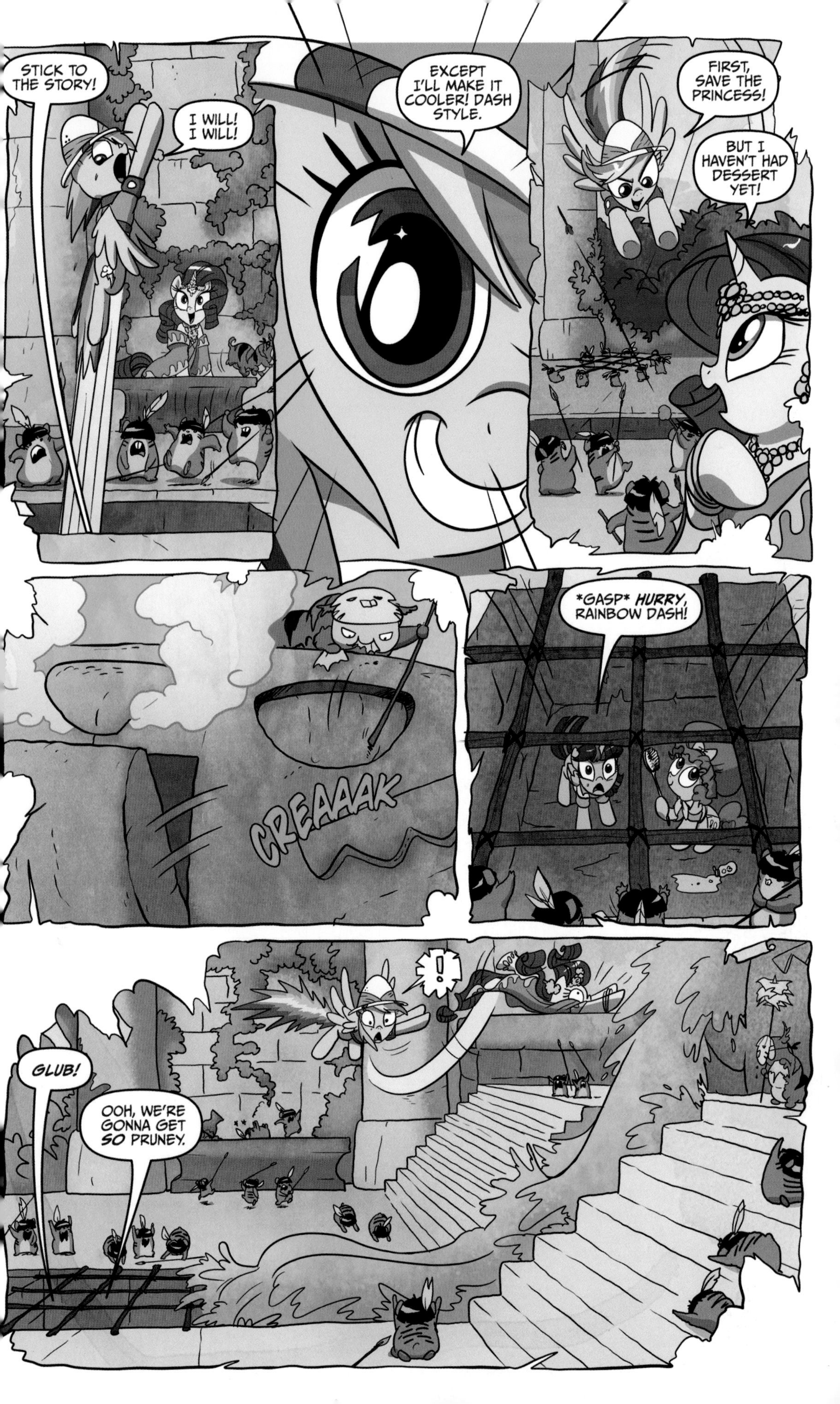

STICK TO THE STORY!
I WILL! I WILL!
EXCEPT I'LL MAKE IT COOLER! DASH STYLE.
FIRST, SAVE THE PRINCESS!
BUT I HAVEN'T HAD DESSERT YET!
CREAAAK
GASP HURRY, RAINBOW DASH!
!
GLUB!
OOH, WE'RE GONNA GET SO PRUNEY.

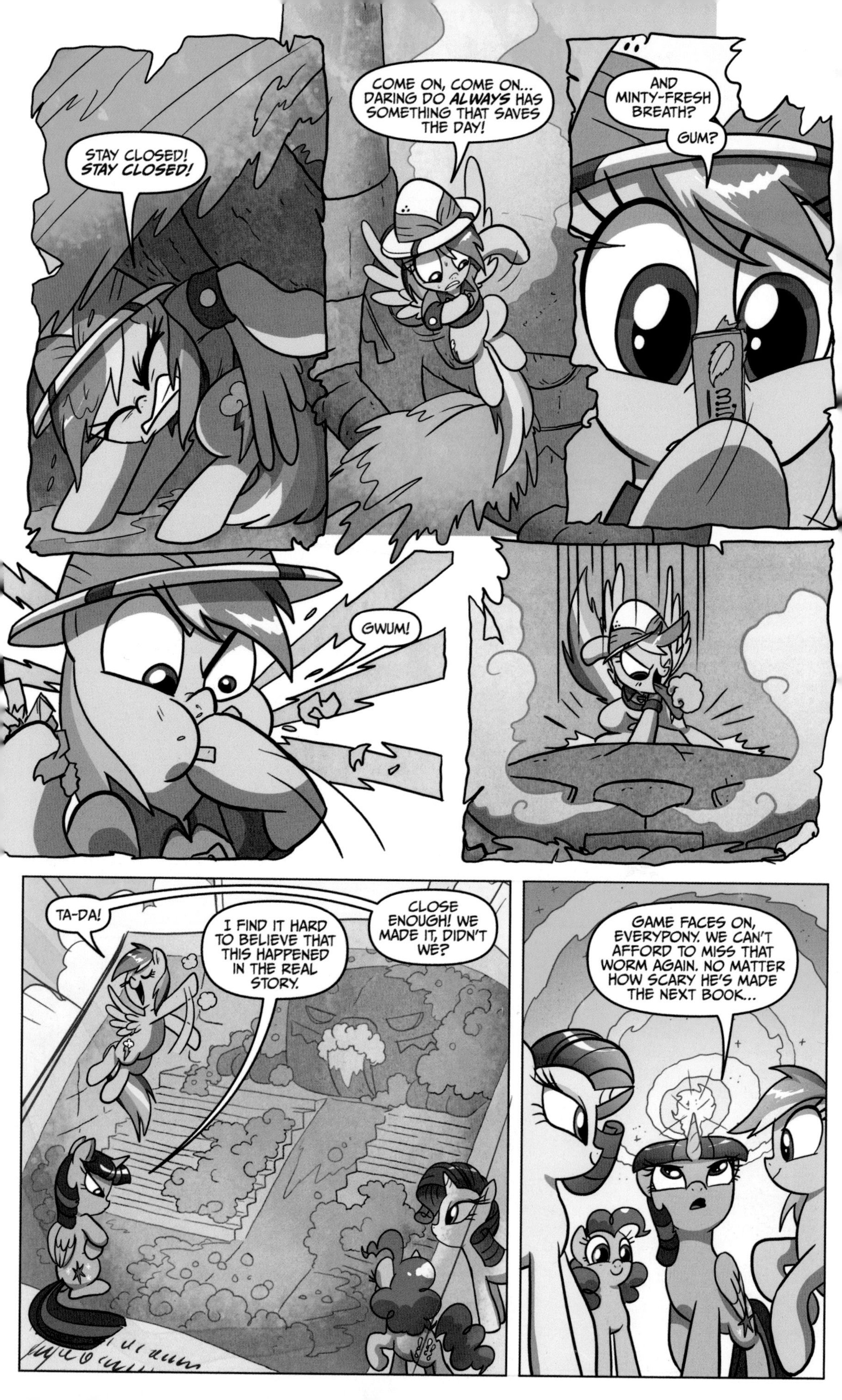
STAY CLOSED! STAY CLOSED!
COME ON, COME ON... DARING DO ALWAYS HAS SOMETHING THAT SAVES THE DAY!
AND MINTY-FRESH BREATH?
GUM?
GWUM!
TA-DA!
I FIND IT HARD TO BELIEVE THAT THIS HAPPENED IN THE REAL STORY.
CLOSE ENOUGH! WE MADE IT, DIDN'T WE?
GAME FACES ON, EVERYPONY. WE CAN'T AFFORD TO MISS THAT WORM AGAIN. NO MATTER HOW SCARY HE'S MADE THE NEXT BOOK...

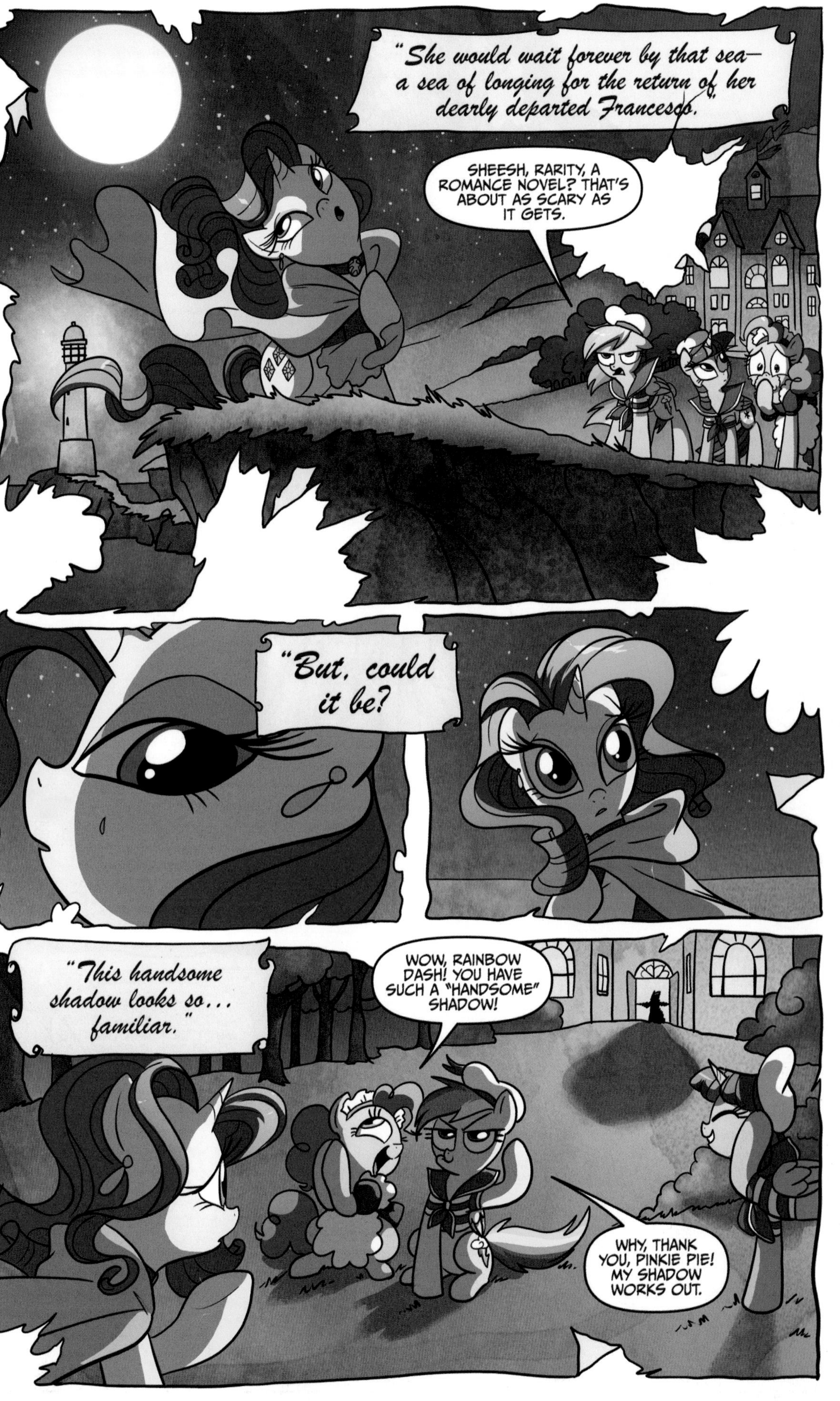
"She would wait forever by that sea— a sea of longing for the return of her dearly departed Francesco."
SHEESH, RARITY, A ROMANCE NOVEL? THAT'S ABOUT AS SCARY AS IT GETS.
"But, could it be?
"This handsome shadow looks so... familiar."
WOW, RAINBOW DASH! YOU HAVE SUCH A "HANDSOME" SHADOW!
WHY, THANK YOU, PINKIE PIE! MY SHADOW WORKS OUT.

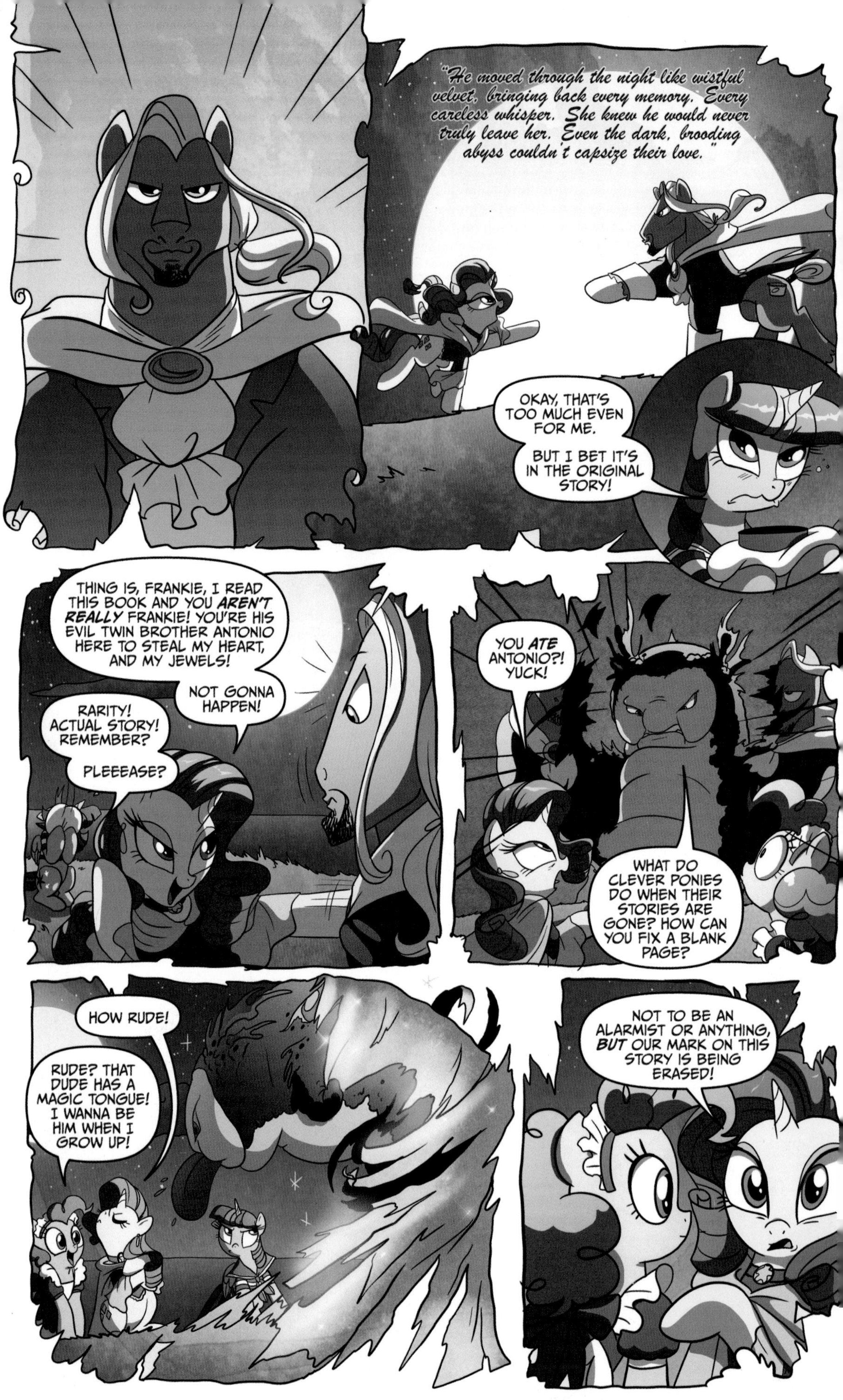
"He moved through the night like wistful velvet, bringing back every memory. Every careless whisper. She knew he would never truly leave her. Even the dark, brooding abyss couldn't capsize their love."
OKAY, THAT'S TOO MUCH EVEN FOR ME.
BUT I BET IT'S IN THE ORIGINAL STORY!
THING IS, FRANKIE, I READ THIS BOOK AND YOU *AREN'T REALLY* FRANKIE! YOU'RE HIS EVIL TWIN BROTHER ANTONIO HERE TO STEAL MY HEART, AND MY JEWELS!
NOT GONNA HAPPEN!
RARITY! ACTUAL STORY! REMEMBER?
PLEEEASE?
YOU *ATE* ANTONIO?! YUCK!
WHAT DO CLEVER PONIES DO WHEN THEIR STORIES ARE GONE? HOW CAN YOU FIX A BLANK PAGE?
HOW RUDE!
RUDE? THAT DUDE HAS A MAGIC TONGUE! I WANNA BE HIM WHEN I GROW UP!
NOT TO BE AN ALARMIST OR ANYTHING, *BUT* OUR MARK ON THIS STORY IS BEING ERASED!

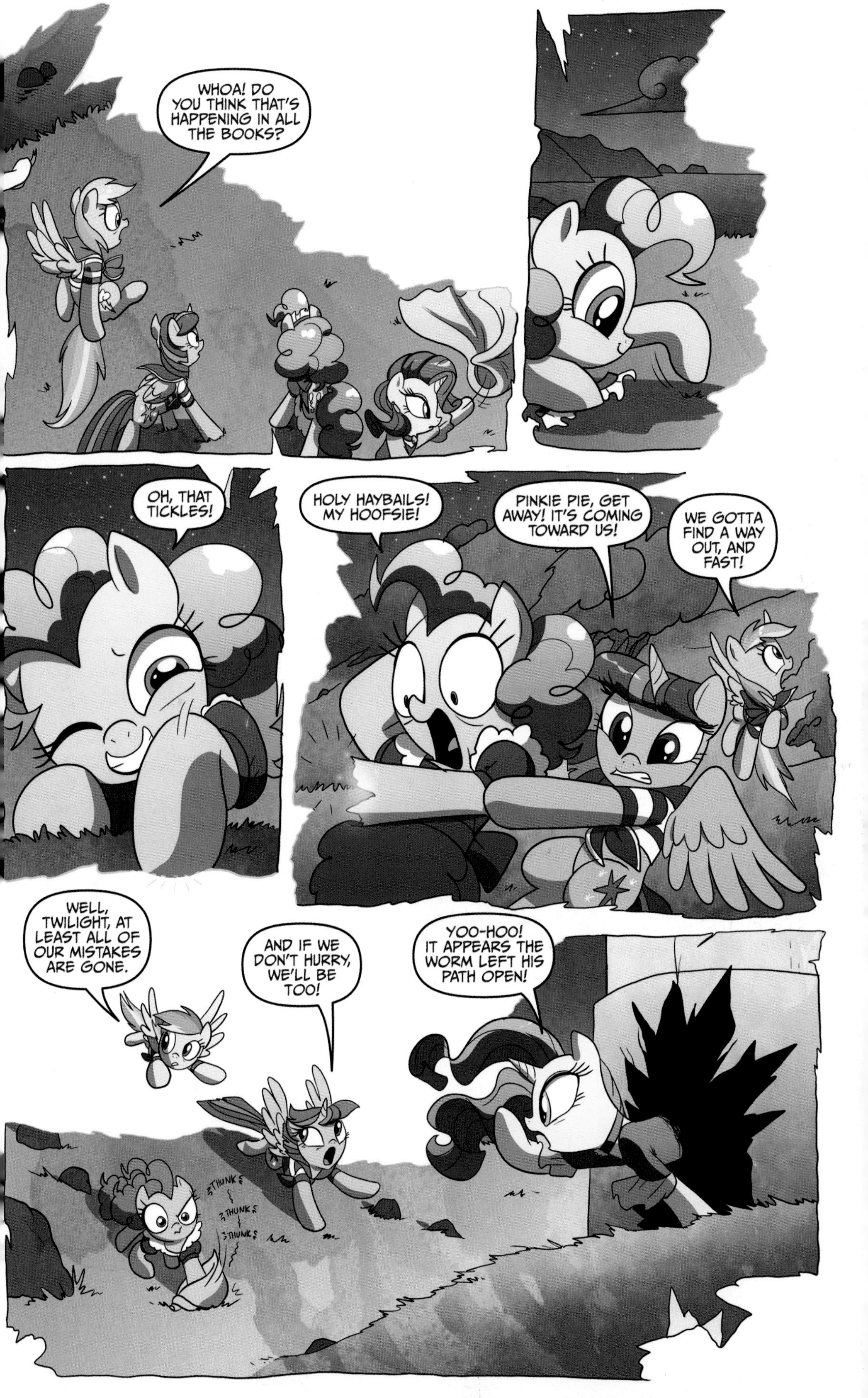

WHOA! DO YOU THINK THAT'S HAPPENING IN ALL THE BOOKS?
OH, THAT TICKLES!
HOLY HAYBAILS! MY HOOFSIE!
PINKIE PIE, GET AWAY! IT'S COMING TOWARD US!
WE GOTTA FIND A WAY OUT, AND FAST!
WELL, TWILIGHT, AT LEAST ALL OF OUR MISTAKES ARE GONE.
AND IF WE DON'T HURRY, WE'LL BE TOO!
YOO-HOO! IT APPEARS THE WORM LEFT HIS PATH OPEN!
THUNK
THUNK
THUNK

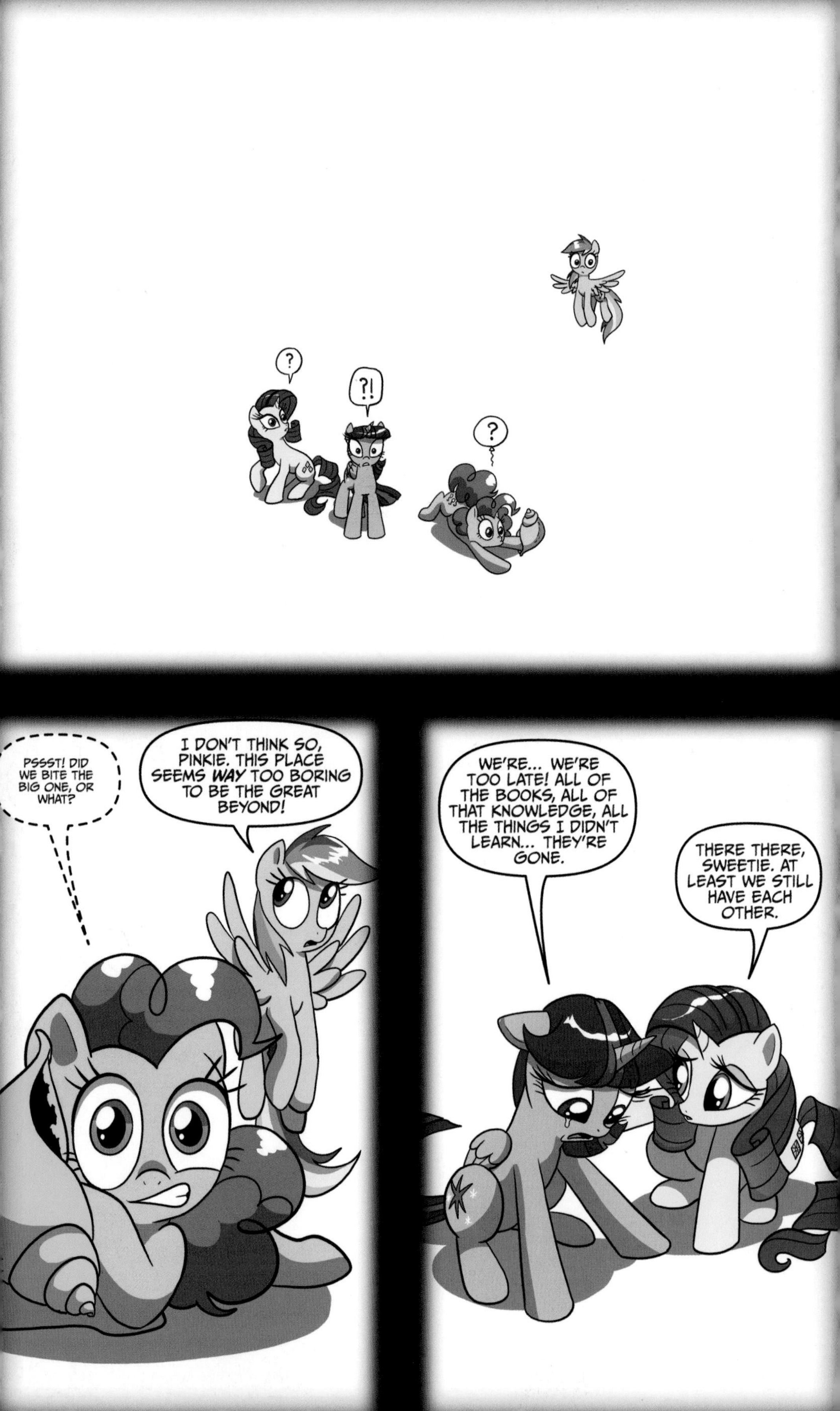

?
?!
?
PSSST! DID WE BITE THE BIG ONE, OR WHAT?
I DON'T THINK SO, PINKIE. THIS PLACE SEEMS *WAY* TOO BORING TO BE THE GREAT BEYOND!
WE'RE... WE'RE TOO LATE! ALL OF THE BOOKS, ALL OF THAT KNOWLEDGE, ALL THE THINGS I DIDN'T LEARN... THEY'RE GONE.
THERE THERE, SWEETIE. AT LEAST WE STILL HAVE EACH OTHER.

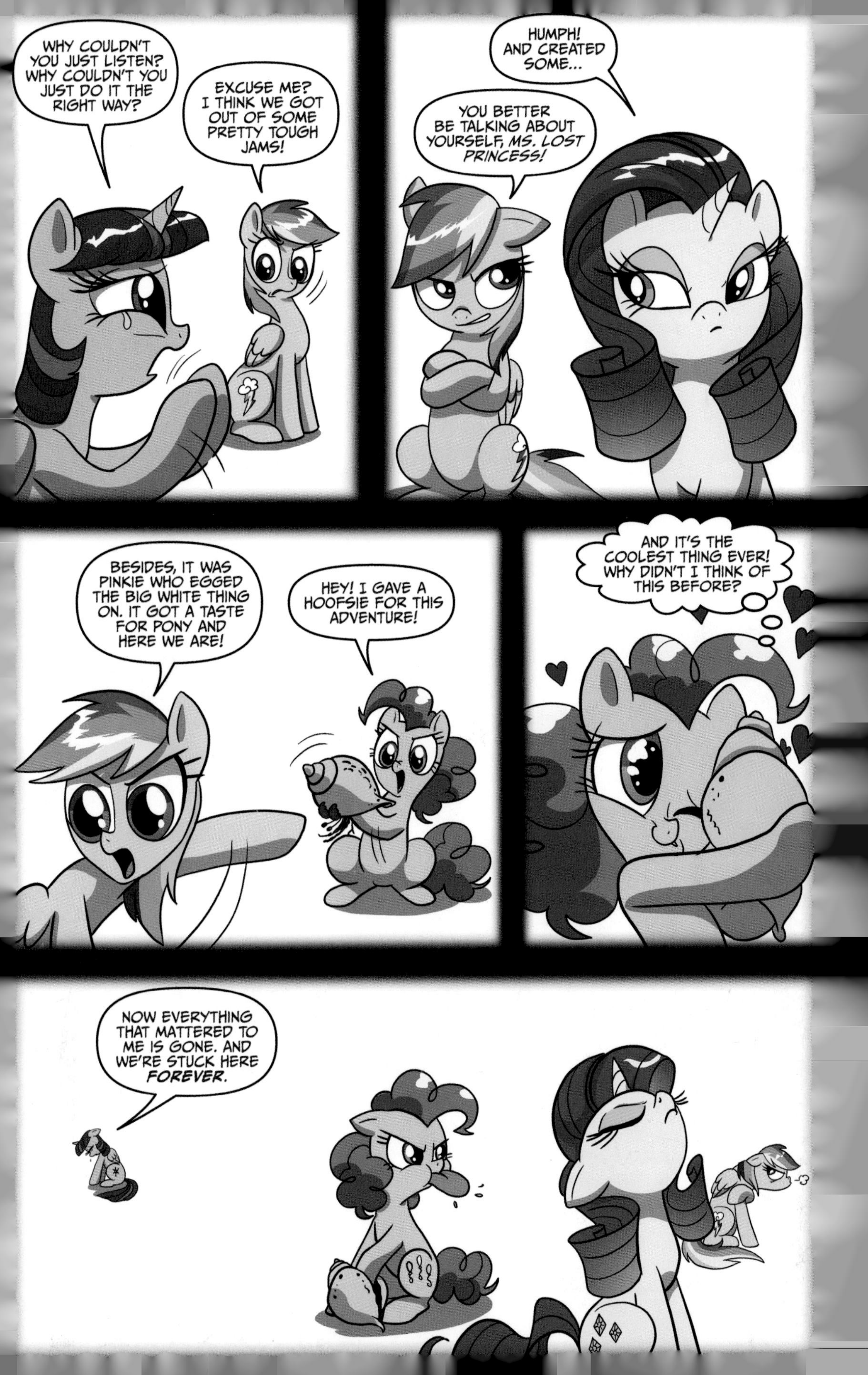
WHY COULDN'T YOU JUST LISTEN? WHY COULDN'T YOU JUST DO IT THE RIGHT WAY?
EXCUSE ME? I THINK WE GOT OUT OF SOME PRETTY TOUGH JAMS!
HUMPH! AND CREATED SOME...
YOU BETTER BE TALKING ABOUT YOURSELF, MS. LOST PRINCESS!
BESIDES, IT WAS PINKIE WHO EGGED THE BIG WHITE THING ON. IT GOT A TASTE FOR PONY AND HERE WE ARE!
HEY! I GAVE A HOOFSIE FOR THIS ADVENTURE!
AND IT'S THE COOLEST THING EVER! WHY DIDN'T I THINK OF THIS BEFORE?
NOW EVERYTHING THAT MATTERED TO ME IS GONE. AND WE'RE STUCK HERE *FOREVER*.

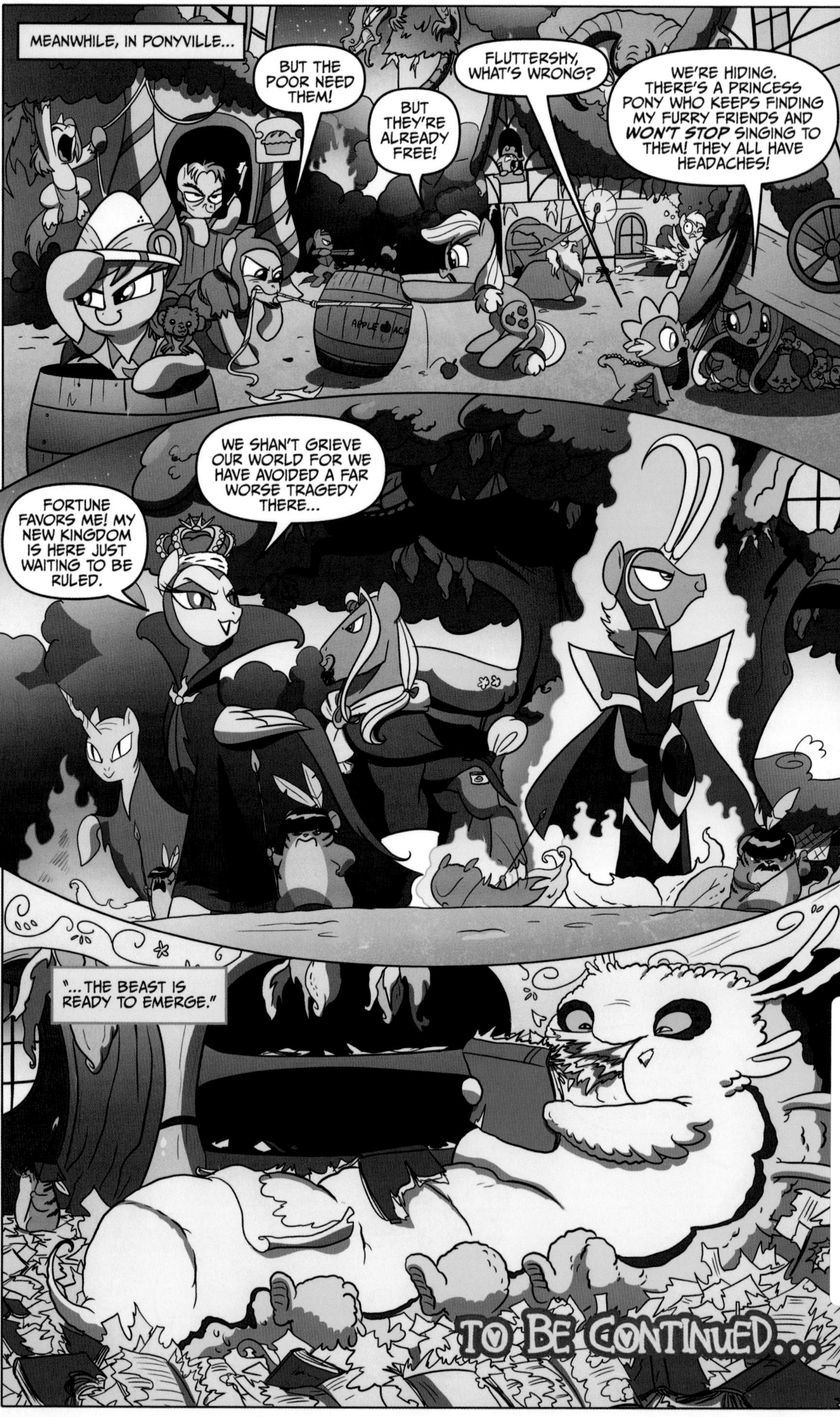
MEANWHILE, IN PONYVILLE...
BUT THE POOR NEED THEM!
BUT THEY'RE ALREADY FREE!
FLUTTERSHY, WHAT'S WRONG?
WE'RE HIDING. THERE'S A PRINCESS PONY WHO KEEPS FINDING MY FURRY FRIENDS AND WON'T STOP SINGING TO THEM! THEY ALL HAVE HEADACHES!
FORTUNE FAVORS ME! MY NEW KINGDOM IS HERE JUST WAITING TO BE RULED.
WE SHAN'T GRIEVE OUR WORLD FOR WE HAVE AVOIDED A FAR WORSE TRAGEDY THERE...
"...THE BEAST IS READY TO EMERGE."
TO BE CONTINUED...